# HARBINGER OF DEATH

Tia Cherie Polite

To the Polite, Walker, Habteab, Baker and Jones families… my BLOOD.
To my friends in the "DMV" and beyond… my CLAN.

*... I must warn you. If you do this, War will come, but it will not come alone. For there can be no war without Death.*

**- Seer to Revanche**

# 1

On Earth, they would be called vampires. Undead creatures of the night with sharp fangs who consume blood. But this isn't Earth. This is the planet Polemis. And these aren't vampires, they are the Nisha.

The Nisha are a clan of night worshippers. They inhabit the southern region of Polemis. Riding on giant nocturnal mammals called Petaurus, the sinewy gray hued beings hunt at night, avoid sunlight and wear mouth harnesses with metal fangs dipped in a parasitic poison. Their diet is fresh fish, wild boar... and blood. The blood of the beings they've chosen to hunt for the past seven nights is that of another clan inhabiting the same region, the Indali.

The Indali are nothing like the Nisha. They share the same long lifespans as all born on Polemis do, but that is where the similarities end. Although not exact, the closest comparison to the Indali on Earth would be of the ancient and noble class of Samurai warrior with their fearsome array of weapons. Or perhaps the fierce Maasai warriors of Kenya would be a better comparison as the Indali share both their beautiful dark skin and ferocious fighting skills. Or maybe even the Scottish

Highlanders with their similar leadership structure and battle charge strategy.

But we are not on Earth, we are on Polemis, and on Polemis even the closest comparison doesn't fully describe the Indali... especially their mightiest warrior.


Volana, Osupa and Marana, the three moons of Polemis, hang ominously in the night sky, providing the only visible source of light.

A flock of tiny white-winged creatures called Skyfish fly high above as they make their quinquennial flight across Polemis to their spawning grounds on the other side of the planet. Their route tonight takes them over Sanguinos, the present-day fortress home of the Indali known as Indali City.

On top of one of the Indali fortresses' battlements, a powerfully built Indali warrior clad in blue and gold armor scans the dark battlefield. He has maintained this ready position, longbow and arrow in hand, ready to fire, since dusk as he watches and waits. He sees nothing yet, but he knows they're coming. They always come.

His eye twitches slightly as he sees movement in the distance. The absence of light makes this movement imperceptible to any of his three-thousand fellow Indali warriors guarding the gates of the city below. Then he hears it. No one else can hear it yet, but he can. That unmistakable sound of high-pitched squeaks growing louder and louder. He launches his arrow and tracks it as it disappears into the night sky. Moments later, a slight flash on the ground, fifteen-hundred-foot lengths away, shows the arrow has found its intended mark. The area illuminates for all to see. Twenty-five hundred Nisha warriors approaching fast. It's down from the more than four thousand Nisha when the raids started, but after six consecutive nights of dusk to dawn battle, even the most battle-hardened warriors' nerves and bodies show signs of wear.

Still, the Indali warriors ready themselves to once again defend their city.

The powerfully built warrior puts down his longbow and picks up a signaling flag. He signals for the archers to nock their arrows and stand ready to fire. The archers pull out red spark crystal tipped arrows from the quivers strapped to their backs.

The powerfully built warrior signals for the archers to fire. The archers' arrows whistle as they disappear into the night sky. The skill of the archers is clear as the arrows reach their ground targets. The loud wail of the approaching arrows disorients The Nisha moments before the bright flash and loud bang of explosions as the arrows strike the spark crystal laced grounds the Nisha are standing on. Nisha bodies are flung in the air and ripped to shreds by the explosions. Those unfortunate to be in physical contact with the crystals when they spark are instantly incinerated.

Several volleys of arrows manage to trim the Nisha numbers, but more than enough remain. The survivors advance quickly, eager to sink their blades and fangs into Indali flesh.

Leading the Indali into battle is the wise veteran Indali warrior, General Taan.

"Shields up, swords ready!" General Taan says to his warriors as he draws the famed golden sword, Halcyondis.

The Indali warriors follow his command.

"To the last!!!" said General Taan as he and his warriors run into battle.

Sword meets shield as the Indali and Nisha warriors clash in a symphony of steel. The battlefield soon becomes a wasteland of severed heads and limbs. The ear-piercing screams of the wounded make for a frightening sound.

Fighting amidst this storm of metal and flesh is the same powerfully built warrior who was previously on top of the battlement. After signaling for the archers to fire, he hung his bow across his body, unsheathed his sword and leaped fifty-foot lengths to the ground to join the battle without ever breaking stride. An impossible distance for any known human to safely traverse unaided. Even on Polemis, this is clearly no ordinary warrior. This is a warrior unlike any Polemis has ever seen. A common saying among the Indali is "There are warriors... and then there is Thane." Strong. Fast. Intelligent. Fearless. Thane's deep brown eyes, with their subtle bits of yellow, can see as well as the best birds of prey, and his strength is better than that of three men at their physical and athletic peak. He fights like he was born for this. Some believe he was born for this. His father was the revered Indali Chieftain, Revanche. His mother was the sword master, strategist and Indali War Chief, Kytara.

Thane's sword continuously finds its mark as he fights his way over to stand back-to-back with General Taan. "Commander Thane my boy," said General Taan, "how soon until dawn arrives to once again drive these cursed demons from our gates?"

"Six hundred twenty tics." replies Thane.

This would equate to roughly ten hours on Earth. On Polemis, with its thirty-hour days, this equates to just over fifteen hours.

General Taan gores a charging Nisha warrior. "Ack, too long. These attacks have taken their toll. For every Nisha we kill, we lose twice that number to their poisoned fangs and chain-blades. I fear we may not hold our ground this night."

General Taan makes a quick visual survey of the battlefield. To his left he witnesses a pair of Indali spearwomen impressively take down a group of Nisha attackers. General Taan fathoms he has been in more battles than most of the warriors under him combined. He glances to his right and sees several Indali swordsmen, some he's known for many moons, lying dead from various fatal wounds. He realizes he's also seen more friends die during those battles than anyone ever should.

General Taan makes a tactical decision to deploy his best asset in a new way.

"We need to drive a stake through the heart of their lines."

He looks over his shoulder at Thane. "Go raise havoc."

Thane nods and makes eye contact with two of his fellow commanders and friends, Ayanti and Leto. Thane leads them, and a dozen other warriors, as they cut and slash their way through hordes of Nisha.

Kor'vai, the ancient and diminutive Nisha brood Queen, looks up from sinking her metal fangs into a convulsing Indali warrior and sees Thane leave his defensive position. A veteran battlefield tactician in her own right, Kor'vai sees the opening she's been waiting for. She hisses and communicates to her warriors in their Nish language *"Now!!!"*. A small cadre of Nisha create a phalanx around Kor'vai, hiding her as they make their way through the swarm of bodies and blades towards their intended target.

Thane and his unit carve a path through the Nisha lines, dividing them as they go. Thane's superior speed, strength and reflexes allow him to act as the tip of a spear and take on the brunt of the attack. Ayanti positions herself just behind Thane's right shoulder, taking out attackers to her right while Leto does the same on Thane's left. The other Indali with them cover the rear as they move.

The group complete their path through. Thane pulls two spark crystals from his waist. He tosses one high in the air, then throws the other one at it, creating a bright spark.

General Taan withdraws his sword from the just disemboweled remains of a Nisha when he sees the bright spark of the crystals in the night sky.

"That's my boy." General Taan says with pride. He then takes out his signaling horn and blows a series of notes, signaling well drilled battle charge instructions to his warriors.

The Indali warriors quickly form up and change from their previous defensive deployment to one more offensive to attack the now divided lines of the Nisha.

The change in battle strategy works as the Nisha lose ground to the pressing Indali attack.

Thane's group fans out to attack the Nisha at will. He manages to get a view of General Taan as he fights. He sees his friend and mentor and smiles, assured that victory will be theirs once again.

Thane's victorious expression changes to one of horror as he sees Kor'vai appear behind General Taan. She sinks her sharp metal fangs into General Taan's neck. Blood from his jugular vein sprays into Kor'vai's mouth and runs down her throat.

"NOOOOOOO!!!" Thane screams in horror.

For the briefest of moments, Thane's dark brown eyes momentarily take on a yellow and amber colored tint before returning to their normal shade.

The Nisha swarm Thane as he tries to make his way to General Taan. He chops them down left and right as he moves. The ones his blade cannot reach, he snares in his vice like grip. Their throats are crushed and their dead bodies flung aside like sacks of grain. Those that are able to sink their metal fangs into Thanes' bare arms are introduced to the revelation that piercing his skin is nigh impossible. Their fangs crack and shatter like glass without drawing even the tiniest drop of blood. Without breaking stride, Thane grabs the Nisha around its throat and lifts him high in the air. The Nisha gasps and struggles. Thane releases and beheads him with his sword as he falls. Despite his furious rampage, there are still just too many of them for Thane to dispatch and still reach his General in time.

General Taan feels the life rapidly draining from him as the parasitic poison and blood loss strain his body. Despite his dire situation, General Taan still manages to gather enough remaining strength and will to wield Halcyondis for one last act. He thrusts Halcyondis into Kor'vai's side. Her jaws release their vice like grip and she howls in pain. General Taan whirls Halcyondis around and decapitates her.

Thane arrives and catches General Taan as he falls to the ground. The grief in Thane's eyes is heartbreaking.

"Do it." General Taan orders. "Let me die as I lived, not as the withered shell I'll soon be."

Thane stares mournfully at his commander, friend and surrogate father figure. General Taan clasps Thane's arm.

"Hurry before it's too..."

General Taan begins convulsing. As the parasite filled poison rapidly makes its way through his bloodstream, General Taan's formerly firm dark skin begins turning grey and withered. His toned athletic physique rapidly takes on a gaunt appearance.

General Taan's withering arm trembles as he tries to hand Halcyondis to Thane. The blade slips out of his hand, but Thane catches it before it hits the ground.

General Taan strains out as his final order. "The field is yours."

Thane stands. He backs away a short distance, pulling two arrows with crystal tips out of the quiver strapped to his back as he walks.

General Taan smiles tenderly at Thane and hoarsely whispers his final words. "Your mother and father would have been so proud of the man and warrior you've become. As have I."

Thane nocks the arrows and fires. They fly through the air and strike together just before hitting General Taan. They spark and incinerate the legendary General. Thane drops his bow and looks down at Halcyondis. He grips the hilt tightly with both hands. A large group of Nisha approach fast. Thane turns to look at them with madness in his eyes.


The darkness of night begins to give way as dawn approaches. In the bloodiest night of the raids, the Indali warriors, led by a grief and rage, fueled Thane, slaughter many Nisha and manage to keep the blood thirsty warriors outside the walls of Indali city for yet another night. The Nisha were simply unable to overcome the loss of their Queen Kor'vai, as the Indali did with their loss of General Taan. One of the Nisha emits a high-pitched wail through their battle horn, signaling their retreat. Their Petaurus's hear the call and swoop in. The Nisha leap to grab harnesses strapped to the flying creatures. With their leader dead, and their numbers severely dwindling, the Nisha finally had enough. They fly off to their caves in defeat.

The Indali warriors enter the city gates as heroes, but many are in bad shape. They are tended to by the denizens of the city. Various plant herbs are used to help ward off infection then bound in strips of cloth. Teams of volunteers venture outside the gates with water and reams of cloth to wash and wrap the bodies of the Indali dead before setting them ablaze atop small makeshift pyres.

The commanders are summoned to the Indali castle to meet with Kotoru, the Indali Chieftain and Thane's uncle.

The N'Dal, the personal guards of Chieftain Kotoru, stand guard at all entrances to the Throne Room. Kotoru's creation of his own personal guard, a decision highly justifiable in Kotoru's eyes given the state of Polemis at the time, never sat right with General Taan, recalls Thane as he enters the Throne Room. The modest Indali Throne Room, along with the castle, fortress and city, was built during a very different time on Polemis by a very different occupant. A well-deserved spoil from a bloody war after a hundred millennia of persecution, forced displacement and genocide, General Taan and other Indali victors would say.

The twenty-seven surviving commanders take their seats in two long facing rows. As holder of General Taan's golden sword, Thane gives the after-battle report.

"We lost over five hundred warriors this night. This puts our total losses since the raids began at over fourteen hundred. We estimate Nisha losses at over twenty-three hundred. It will take them many moons to increase their numbers to their previous levels. Since they only like to initiate prolonged attacks at full strength, they won't threaten us again for some time."

Listening intently from his throne sits a stout and grizzled older man with calculating eyes.

Thane unsheathes Halcyondis and presents it to Kotoru.

"He fought bravely until the end." Thane proudly proclaims.

Kotoru regards Thane for a moment before taking
the sword.

"I'm sure he did, commander Thane."

Kotoru locks eyes with all of his commanders.

"You have proven valiant in the face of darkness and saved us from it. All of Indali City thanks you. Go home to your families. Rest and relax, for tonight we celebrate."

The commanders touch their right fists to their hearts and honorably bow to their chieftain. They turn to leave when Kotoru speaks again.

"A moment of your time, Commander Thane."

"We will wait for you outside." Ayanti tells Thane.

Thane approaches Kotoru's throne and kneels.

"Our nights of terror seem to be at an end." Kotoru says.

Thane slowly nods his head, but doesn't speak. Kotoru looks at his nephew with soft eyes.

"How are you?" Kotoru asks.

"I am well. I suffered no injuries."

Kotoru smiles warmly and motions for Thane to rise.

"I mourn your loss. I know how much Taan meant to you."

Thane's sorrowful eyes look away.

Kotoru gets down from his throne and walks over to place his hand on Thane's shoulder. "I, too, share the agony of your loss. He was... an outstanding and distinguished warrior and General. He will be missed."

"He will indeed." replies Thane.

Kotoru gently guides Thane to walk with him.

"The senior commanders speak highly of your actions on the battlefield."

"Thank you, uncle. Every warrior fought valiantly through many difficult battles."

"And thus, we will honor them tonight with feast and wine."

says Kotoru.

"They would enjoy that." replies Thane.

Kotoru stops. "But not you?"

Thane stops and turns to his uncle with a lackluster smile. "As the young ones say, it is not my type of thing."

Kotoru chuckles lightly at Thanes' remark.

"Nevertheless, your chieftain expects you there this evening."

Thane stiffens. "Then I shall be."

Kotoru unsheathes Halcyondis and takes a long look at it.

"With your father's sword lost to time, this is the most recognizable symbol of Indali might still in our people's possession."

Kotoru runs his finger along the names of the Indali War Chiefs etched along the blade in the ancient nomadic language of the clans known as Kalayman. Other than its appearance on some ancient cave walls and artifacts, it is pretty much a dead language on Polemis.

Kotoru continues running his finger along the modern language names. The last three are Revanche, Kytara, and Taan. Kotoru glares at Kytara's name.

"When your father chose your mother as his War Chief, it ended a long tradition of our blood kin that extend as far back as our great ancestor and clan founder Indala choosing his younger brother Anon as the first War Chief."

Kotoru's lips pull inward as he recalls a memory. "Your skills would be better served as Vanguard, guardian and governor of our villages, he told me. Thus, I was elsewhere when the Blood Nobles launched their vicious surprise attack, killing your mother. Seeing your father's grief was agonizing. His decision to surrender to the Nobles for execution in exchange for ending the war was the most heartbreaking display of heroism I had ever seen. It was then that I found out my brother wanted me to lead this clan as Chieftain in his absence."

Kotoru stands tall. "And so I have."

Kotoru takes a last look at Halcyondis. He sheathes the sword and hands it back to Thane.

"I am entrusting this to you until I have chosen our new War Chief."

Thane takes the sword.

"Until this evening, young nephew."

Thane bows to his uncle. "Until this evening uncle."

As Thane leaves the throne room, Kotoru smirks as he watches Thane with a curious mixture of amusement tinged with contempt.

Outside the castle, Thane is in a dour mood when he meets up with Ayanti and Leto.

"Wouldn't let you out of celebration tonight, would he?" Leto asks. Thane grits his teeth.

Leto thrusts his arms in the air. "Fight. Win. Drink. Eat. Celebrate. And hope you live long enough to do it all over again many times. The life of a warrior." Leto's deep baritone voice carries his words to all within earshot. The warriors who hear it say the words along with Leto.

"Fight to live... then do the living." says Leto.

Thane's mood begins to lift. His mood brightens even more when he spots a hooded figure dressed in a simple beige tunic and pants hiding in the shadows near the city stables, waving him over. Thane turns to Ayanti and Leto, grinning like a big kid. He starts to speak, but Ayanti beats him to it.

"Have fun." she says. Thane runs off towards the stables. Leto laughs and shakes his head.

"Who else could battle a vicious horde of blood sucking, sword wielding night terrors and still have the energy left for that."

Through the mountainous lands that cover the southern region of Polemis, Thane rides his powerful red steedar, Perangun hard and fast. The tail-less four-legged riding animal with sharp bones protruding from its head and body enjoys the opportunity to stretch its legs almost as much as Thane. They are truly kindred spirits. The only creature who enjoys it more than this pair is the hooded two-legged one quickly gaining on them. What this creature lacks in grace it more than makes up for in determination.

Thane feels the creature gaining on him. He smiles and whistles a tune into Perangun's ear that communicates Thane's desire for him to run faster. The red steedar readily obliges and accelerates to its top speed. They surge ahead of the hooded creature. Thane approaches the end of a cliff and whistles for Perangun to stop. Perangun stops, and Thane jumps down. He walks over to the edge of the cliff and kneels down. He estimates it's well over eight-hundred-foot lengths to the rocky bottom.

The hooded creature silently walks up next to Thane and kneels down beside him. They both look across to the other side that is at least sixty-foot lengths across. It is a distance no being or creature known on land should ever be able to make. The two exchange looks. Thane walks back about fifteen-foot lengths. He takes a deep breath, then runs forward and leaps off the cliff. Thane's incredible speed, strength and agility allow him to sail through the air across the wide chasm. He lands hard, rolling over his shoulder up onto one knee on the other side of the cliff. Thane gets up and dusts himself off.

Thane walks over to a nearby tree and pulls off a piece of wild fruit. He sniffs it then looks back across the deep chasm. Thane holds up and waves the wild fruit while whistling a tune for Perangun. Perangun brays joyfully and quickly takes off running to find one of the mountain passages to the tasty meal waiting for him on the other side.

Thane turns his attention to the hooded figure.

"You coming?"

The hooded figure runs back to the same spot Thane did, then runs forward and leaps off the cliff. The form is less polished. Less clean. Less powerful. Nevertheless, the hooded figure sails through the air and approaches the other side. It's at this point both the hooded figure and Thane realize the jump is going to be short. Several foot lengths short, in fact. At the last moment, Thane reaches out and grabs the hooded figure's arm. He then swings them up over the ledge.

"Still looking out for me dear brother." says the hooded figure in a young woman's voice.

Thane smiles and says, "Always last born."

The hooded figure removes her hood, revealing a young woman with yellow eyes and amber-colored irises that look more animalistic than human. Several places on her face, arms and legs are marked with various gray-colored hard-shell scabs. Healed over remnants from assorted severe injuries. She is Syn, Thane's twin sister.

"Only by one tic, first born." Syn replies.


Inside a room known as the "Room of the Chieftains" filled with historic and personal items of past Indali leaders, Kotoru takes a leisurely stroll admiring the various items. Trailing behind him is his long-time aide and advisor, Rattan.

Kotoru stops and gazes at a rendering commemorating the Battle of Sangmoria, the final battle of the Blood War where the Blood Nobles were defeated on what is now Indali City. Pictured prominently in the rendering is the man who led that battle, General Taan, pointing Halcyondis at what used to be called Sangmoria Palace. Kotoru laughs.

Although Kotoru is very much relieved that the threat of the Nisha has finally passed, a not so insignificant part of his joy is a death that took place during the battle.

"General Taan. The last of my brothers' sycophants is finally dead." Kotoru says. "This is truly a glorious day indeed.

Perhaps now I can finally rule my clan as I see fit without one of my dead brother's minions hovering over me. Questioning my every order".

"As it should be, my lord.", Rattan adds.

Kotoru walks over to a mantle. Over top of the mantle hang renderings of former Indali Chieftains. Kotoru regards each one as he walks, stopping at the one of his brother Revanche, holding the ancient Indali Leadership Sword and leading his people into battle. Kotoru takes down the painting and stares at it.

"As much as I loved my brother, he was a fool who got in over his head with his revolution against the Blood Nobles and... got what he deserved. All of them did." Kotoru grows angry thinking about them.

"Kytara, who failed to know her place and thought herself my better. Seer, the blind girl who filled my brother's head with visions of delusion. Vorii, the angry orphan girl begging for revenge who followed my brother around like a lost baby steedar begging to be petted. Rukai. Me'nar. Lokeer. Bor. Sateea." Kotoru exhales deeply and places the rendering back on the mantle. "But that is ancient history. It is time for me to lead us into our future and gain true power the likes the Indali have never seen."

"The Three Moons." Rattan says.

"The Rohini." says Kotoru. "They show us the way to the future. Rule not on the ground with swords and spears, but through the air with mighty ships and weapons. I just need to convince Lord Kazini and the other Three Moons lords that all the old vendettas died with General Taan."

"What about Taan's own disciples? One rather large and powerful one in particular?"

"Thane." says Kotoru.

"He is fated to unite the clans and lead us to victory over our greatest enemy. Lord Revanche decreed it himself.", Rattan reminds his Chieftain.

"His son is nothing more than an overgrown boy who would rather run the lands of Polemis with his useless abomination of a sister than rule. It's just as well, though. He would no doubt let his foolish ideals lead us to the same fate as his father.". An idea comes to Kotoru. "Unless I use those ideals against him." Kotoru's lips curve into a wicked smile. "Why not."

"Why not what my lord?" asks a confused Rattan.

"Make him my War Chief." Kotoru delightedly answers.

"My lord?", Rattan asks still perplexed as to his Chieftain's plan.

"Even before Taan gave him field command before he died, he already had the respect of the other commanders."

Kotoru continues laying out his rationale. "The mere suggestion of an alliance with the Rohini would have meant Taan's blade at my throat with the backing of every commander and warrior in his ranks. Thane is different. Duty. Honor. Loyalty. They have been the focus of so much of Taan's teachings that he would rather walk away completely than raise his sword against his chieftain. That makes him controllable."

"But... what of the more senior commanders? Are they not more ready and deserving?", Rattan counters.

"They will obey the commands of their chieftain."

Rattan remains unconvinced. "How will you ensure he will obey your commands?"

Kotoru walks and contemplates that question for a long moment. He stops and turns to Rattan with a most devious smile on his face.

"His sister. Perhaps she isn't so useless after all. If he fails to obey me, if he fails to rollover when I pull his leash, I simply need to pull hers harder."

Rattan is almost incredulous in his reply.

"But she is your niece. Despite your feelings towards her, she is still clan royalty."

Kotoru pulls a knife from a sheath hanging from his belt and turns sharply on Rattan. He presses the knife into Rattan's throat deep enough to draw blood. Rattan's eyes go wide as Kotoru pulls him close. Kotoru looks at Rattan with madness in his eyes. "My dream is for the Indali to have a seat at the Three Moons table... for me to have a seat of power... and I will obliterate anyone who stands in my way, clan or no clan, blood or no blood. Is that clear?" Kotoru says menacingly.

"Of course, my lord. I spoke in error.", Rattan says, quivering. Kotoru releases Rattan. He stares at the blood on his knife before wiping it on Rattan's sleeve and placing the knife back in
its sheath.

"I believe there is a celebration tonight that needs
your attention."

Rattan stammers. "Y-yes my Lord."

"And see to your shirt. We have an image to maintain." Rattan hurriedly leaves, leaving Kotoru to bask in the self-professed glory of his master plan.


High in the mountains, Perangun nibbles on wild fruit while Syn and Thane are able to sit and catch up with each other for the first time since the Nisha attacks began.

"Do it." asks Syn.

"No, it feels weird."

"Do...it."

Thane exasperatedly gives in. "Fine."

Thane closes his eyes and concentrates. When he opens them, they are yellow and amber like his twin sisters. He focuses on a small garden in the distance. There, he sees a pair of fuzzy objects moving around. Thane focuses on them. The fuzzy objects begin to come more into focus. They begin to look like fuzzy people. One of the fuzzy people picks up something from the garden and look at it. Thane concentrates and focuses harder. Beads of sweat collect on Thane's forehead. His eyes start blinking rapidly.

"Ok that's enough". Thane closes his eyes. They revert to their normal dark brown. He blinks several times and shakes his head. "It makes my head hurt to do that."

"What did you see?"

"I saw... Gijann, one of our archers. Has the sides of her head shaved and etched with black ink. She's walking with her mate Wataya. They are picking rain flowers."

Syn takes a look in the same direction. She sees the garden and the two figures in it with almost double the visual acuity of her brother. The same figures that looked fuzzy to Thane appear perfectly clear to Syn. What she sees makes her giggle and causes her to put her hand over her mouth.

"What?" Thane asks.

"It's Gijann alright, but that isn't Wataya she's with and they definitely aren't picking flowers. I win."

"Ok, your eyes definitely still see farther and clearer than mine can, but at least now we know why and how. If I can learn to hold focus, I can catch up some."

Syn taps her cheek with a finger. "So, what's the count now? You're stronger than me."

"Way stronger." Thane adds.

"And you can't get hurt...yet."

Thane playfully scowls at Syn.

"But I'm faster and have better ears, eyes and nose." Syn adds.

"Slightly better... for now."

Thane thinks for a minute. "You know with a little training you'd make the perfect scout. You could keep an eye on the enemy and report back without ever leaving our region."

Syn gets up and walks over to Perangun. She takes notice of Halcyondis hanging from Peragun's saddle. She starts to touch it but stops herself and turns to Thane. He looks around then smiles and nods his permission.

Syn slowly draws Halcyondis just enough to see the last three names. She tenderly touches the names of Revanche and Kytara.

"What's war like?" Syn asks.

Thane contemplates Syn's question for a moment. "General Taan once described war as a necessity for survival when reason and compromise fail to achieve peace."

Syn sheathes Halcyondis and turns to her brother. "That why you like it?"

Thane sighs. "It's not so much that I like it as much as it's something I seem to be very good at. Something I feel I was born to do."

Thane stands and draws his battle sword. He beams as he holds it out in front of himself gripping it tightly.

"When I rush into battle, sword in hand, I feel master of my world. Like nothing ever created can defeat me and all that stand against me will meet their end."

Syn looks up at Thane with a raised eyebrow. Thane chuckles sheepishly and sheaths his sword.

He sits back down. "I guess I do like it... a lot"

Syn sighs heavily. "I wonder what I--"

Syn interrupts herself mid-sentence. She hears something and looks around. Thane hears it several micro-tics later. Had there been anyone with them, that person would have been wondering what they were hearing. It would have been almost another sixty or so micro-tics before the sound would have been close enough to be heard by regular human ears.

"It's them!!!" Syn excitedly exclaims as she jumps up.

"So... top of the mountain?" says Thane.

"Come on!!!" Syn replies as she takes off running.

"Top of the mountain it is." Thane says, before running off after her. Perangun snorts and brays at the pair before returning his attention to his wild fruit buffet.

Riding on Perangun at top speed, Thane would have been almost stride for stride with Syn. On foot, Thane is still faster than any other human, as well as most other animals. Syn, however, is second to none. By the time Thane reaches the top of the mountain, Syn has already settled into viewing position.

Syn can barely contain her excitement.

"Here they come!!!"

The twins look down over the ledge. A convoy of hover ships passes by the mountain forty-foot lengths beneath them. The aging unarmed twenty-three-foot length; multi spin-blade propelled hover ships are believed to be the only known flight capable craft in existence on Polemis. They are the achievement of the largest and most dangerous clan of them all... the Rohini.

The Rohini. Technologically advanced. Powerful. Ruthless. The estimated ninety-thousand strong warrior clan are led by Lord Kazini. Known too many as Kazini the Usurper, he is the fanatical worshipper and scholar of the ancient Polemini moon spirits. Kazini rose to clan lord by executing the entire family of the previous clan chieftain, a clan whose bloodline extended almost as far back as the beginning of civilization on Polemis. Prior to joining the Indali and dozens of other clans to fight the Blood Nobles, the Rohini lived as nomads traveling the grassland regions. They now inhabit Volana, the largest moon of Polemis. Along with their allies, the Niyati and the Satvari, the Rohini gained the technologically advanced Atea City from the Blood Nobles. Together they would use its technology to annex Volana, Osupa and Marama. They left Polemis for the moons and formed a triumvirate called The Almighty Clans of the Three Moons (The Three Moons for short). Collectively, they deny the remaining people of Polemis access to any of their technology.

Syn and Thane continue watching as the convoy of Rohini hover ships fly past them.

"Wow, just look at them." said Syn.

Thane rolls his eyes.

"You sound just like uncle.", he says. Syn ignores her brother.

"You think we'll ever have ships like those?"

"Now you really sound like uncle."

Thane and Syn climb back down the mountain to find Perangun resting after filling his belly with his morning meal.

"What did you mean earlier when you said I sound like uncle?" asks Syn.

"Not long after we first started seeing the Rohini transports, I told uncle. The thought of flying ship thrilled him like nothing else ever had. He had General Taan send scouts to Atea City to try to get a closer look at them and the city."

"What did they see?" Syn asks.

"Not much at first. They saw transports fly into the mouth of a gigantic mountain. They believe this was the entrance to the city itself. Then they saw it. A large platform descending from the sky into the mouth of the mountain. They said it was riding what looked like a metal rope that stretched so far into the sky it looked like it came from the clouds. It was unlike anything they'd ever seen before. They then heard a loud strange voice say 'Space Elevator docking complete.'"

Syn wrinkles her face at Thane.

"What's a Space Elevator?"

"No idea. It's troubling how much more advanced they are than everyone else. Sharing some of their advancements would benefit all of Polemis but instead they hoard it like Sciuridae stockpiling hard fruits for the harsh times."

Syn perceptibly picks up on the concern in her brother's voice.

"If you had some of those ships, you'd be able to fly like the Nisha do."

"No thank you. I'll take a trusty steeder any day over flying." Thane says as he affectionately pats Perangun.


The oncoming mid-day sun brightens the sky as Thane and Syn make the long walk back to Indali city with Perangun.

Syn asks a question that's been on her mind a lot recently.

"You ever think about them, mother and father? I mean, I know we never got to know them, but I still think about them."

"Sometimes. I sometimes wonder what they would think of me. I wonder if father would tell me to make sure the weakest warrior in your ranks is just as capable as your strongest and you'll never go on the battlefield at a disadvantage. I wonder if mother would tell me to keep my sword firm, my mind strong and my heart full."

"What about you?" asked Thane.

Syn hesitates to respond. It's as if she is embarrassed to answer.

"I wonder how they would feel about me. If they would look at me and love me?"

Syn's answer breaks Thane's heart. It's as if this is the first time he's really grasping the depths of his sister's pain. He knows she is not treated well by the people of their city. He knows the same people who revere him largely shun her. He's painfully aware that their uncle Kotoru radiates a simmering dislike of Syn that alternates between disinterest and flat-out hatred for some unknown reason.

He sees the deep sadness in her eyes that she tries to hide behind her lighthearted and curious demeanor. It pains him, but he's unsure what to do about it.

"Well, of course they would. They would be truly taken by their amazing last-born. Just maybe not quite as much as they would their magnificent first born."

Thane couldn't resist playfully poking Syn with his usual joke about their order of birth in the hope that will lighten her mood some. He learns quickly he was not successful.

"I wonder if anyone would even miss me if I weren't here anymore. Assuming they even noticed I was gone. I sometimes wonder why I was ever born."

"Don't talk like that. Chieftain blood runs through your veins same as mine. We must remain strong for one day we will lead this clan."

Syn turns to face her brother. "No, dear brother, one day you will lead this clan. As firstborn, that is your birth right. Your destiny. What is mine? What was I born to do?"

Thane considers for a moment before responding. "Exactly what it will be I cannot say, but whatever your destiny is, it will be one of your choosing."

The answer is not as satisfying as either of them would like it to be. Thane recalls a memory.

"There was this blind woman. An old friend of General Taan. He took me to see her just before he started training me. She lives way out in the desert region. Blind since birth, but always says her eyes have seen more of this world than anyone else will ever see. She told me, 'a person's life tends to play out very much like a book, but that book's beginning won't always be the beginning you want or expect. And that it doesn't stop being written until you get to the end of the last page.'

"So what I'm saying to you is, you will find it in time. It'll probably come out of nowhere and you'll wonder how you could have ever lived so long without it."

Syn considers her twin brother's words as they make their way back home.


It's early afternoon when Syn and Thane return to Indali City. Indali warriors patrolling the entrance of the fortress surrounding the city greet Thane warmly. He makes note of the fact that Syn isn't acknowledged at all.

Inside the gates await two N'Dal.

One of them walks up to Thane. "Lord Kotoru requests your presence."

Thane nods his acknowledgement and turns back to Syn. The N'Dal remain waiting. One of them glares at Syn. She tenses up.

Thane picks up on Syn's tension. He turns and makes eye contact with the N'Dal.

"Anything else?"

The N'Dal turn and leave. When they believe they are a safe distance away, Thane hears one of them whisper a vile remark about Syn, to which the other snickers. Thane considers confronting the pair, but hears General Taan's words in his head about using his strength wisely. Thane decides a more permanent solution is needed.

"I'm going to speak with uncle about how you've been treated and put an end to it."

"You don't need to--"

"I'm also going to tell him I want to bring you in for training."

Syn's eyes grow wide. The ecstasy in Syn's voice is heard by anyone within earshot. "Training! Me! I would... that would

... be great."

Thane smiles and gestures for Syn to reign in her excitement. "It won't be easy, even with your skills. It's going to be a lot of hard work and long hours and I can't show any favoritism to you. You'll have to start with the young ones, but once they see you in action, you'll be a scout warrior in less than six cycles."

The more Thane tells Syn about all the hard parts, the more interested she becomes. The opportunity to not only show what she can do, but to become an accepted and respected member of Indali society, is irresistible to her.

"You really think I can do this." asked Syn.

"I know you can do this. One day when I'm Chieftain and your War Chief and we've restored our clan's honor, we'll have fulfilled father's dream together."

As Thane walks away, Syn calls out to him.

"Thane."

He turns around to her.

"Thank you. Thank you for--"

Thane smiles. "Thank me after you've made it through your first sparring session. Ayanti can be merciless."

As Thane makes his way to the castle to meet with their

uncle, Syn tilts her head back and proudly walks Perangun towards the stables as a lowly stable girl for what she hopes is the last time.

Thane enters the castle and makes his way to the throne room. Upon entering, one of the N'Dal guards escorts him to his uncle's private quarters. That's different., Thane notes to himself. He wonders if his uncle has somehow taken ill. Although the occasional random illness can sometimes occur, outside of serious infection, a fatal injury, widespread disease affecting everyone, or something like the Nisha poison, people born on Polemis rarely get sick. In fact, only people originally born on Polemis are considered long lived and having potential life-spans equal to several millennia on Earth. Those born off-planet on one of the moons have life-spans significantly shorter.

Thane arrives at his uncle's private quarters and is pleased to find him in good health and in even better spirits.

"You summoned me, uncle?"

"Yes, yes, come in." Kotoru says.

Thane enters, and Kotoru motions for him to take a seat.

"Leave us." Kotoru says to his personal attendants who had been dressing him in elaborate robes for the evening celebration.

Thane has never understood his uncle's desire for such pretentiousness. Whether dressing for battle or to break bread, doing so oneself without help was required at all times by General Taan. Hopefully, the new War Chief will continue all of his requirements.

Kotoru admires himself in the highly polished crystal that serves as his mirror. "You will be my War Chief."

Thane fights to keep his mouth from gaping wide at the news.

Kotoru turns to his nephew. "I believe it's still customary to say something when news of this kind is delivered."

"I'm honored. Thank you, uncle."

Kotoru returns his gaze to his mirror posing confidently with his arms clasped behind his back. "Together, we will make the Indali people a force to be reckoned with."

With the momentary shock of his unexpected promotion subsiding, Thane remembers his conversation with Syn and decides the time is now. With his new role as War Chief this should be little more than a formality.

"I agree. In light of that, I would like to make a request."

Kotoru raises an eyebrow. "Already with a request? You don't waste time, do you. Speak your request."

"I would like my sister to begin training and, when she's ready, join our warrior ranks."

Thane might as well have asked his uncle to step down so he could become Chieftain.

Kotoru turns and glares at his nephew.

"No.", said the Indali Chieftain thru sneer twisted lips.

How dare he even think to ask such a question, Kotoru wonders. The thought sickens him. Besides making it near impossible to use Syn to control Thane, and therefore all the Indali Warriors, having her trained as a warrior would be extremely dangerous.

As powerful as Thane is, he has not once ever felt even the slightest bit intimidated by him. Syn, however, is a different story. From the time he first met his brother and Kytara's infant twins, he knew they were different.

One planetary cycle after leaving the Indali village with a small group of followers in search of a young blind girl rumored to have the ability to see future events, Revanche and Kytara returned with ninety-thousand warriors and their chieftains from a coalition of clans, a declaration of war against the Blood Noble Monarchy and two infant twins. The children were a surprise given the last time he spoke to them before they left, they were still grieving the loss of their son Thyrox at the hands of Blood Noble soldiers. From the moment Kotoru looked into Syn's yellow and gold eyes, he felt a shiver he has never felt from anyone else before or since. He felt there was something ominous about her. A sense of malevolence in this infant child he couldn't fully explain. It's a feeling he could never completely shake about her despite her seemingly unassuming nature. When combined alongside the legendary battlefield exploits of Thane, the tales of his incredible feats, and the whispers that he may even be immortal, the pair could become a tremendous threat to him.

Suddenly, a new thought grips his mind like a vice. What if they learned all he'd done in his quest for power. What if they learned of his deal with Lord Kazini to betray the coalition of clans and his plot to take the throne as Chieftain. What if they learned he manipulated their grieving father Revanche into surrendering to the Blood Nobles and face execution. What if they learned it was he who lured their mother Kytara into a trap and killed her.

Kotoru's heart rate increases. His breathing quickens. Beads of sweat form on Kotoru's temples. His mind races as fear takes firm hold of his thoughts. The thought of Thane and Syn united against him...no, he will never allow that to happen.

"I forbid her from ever being trained as a warrior by you or anyone else!!!"

The level of vitriol in Kotoru's voice catches Thane off guard. The thumping of his uncle's heart is like a booming drum in Thane's ears. The putrid smell emanating from his uncle is almost nauseating. Thane can only imagine the amount of unpleasant irritation Syn's senses would be in if she were here right now. He wonders what is it about his sister that could cause this type of reaction in his uncle.

"I don't understand. As War Chief it is my decision as to who may be trained into our ranks."

"And as Chieftain, it is my decision as to what is best for this clan."

Thane remains calm in the face of his uncle's outburst, but knows he must take a stand.

"You are my chieftain and my elder kin. I will obey any just order you give, and what you are asking me to do is not just. She is as much the daughter of a chieftain as you and I are sons. To deny her is to deny her birthright."

Thane's words further enrage his uncle. Kotoru wonders if this is something they've been planning for all along. A dark shutter vibrates through his body and fills his mind with agonizing fear... could she be behind this? Is this her power, to command her brother to act against him?, he wonders. Kotoru chastises himself. Don't be absurd. This is nothing more than a young man testing the boundaries of his newfound authority and he should treat it as such. Kotoru steadies himself. He clasps his hands behind his back and glares at Thane.

"Do not forget your place young nephew."

For a moment, Thane's anger builds at the stinging rebuke. It just as quickly subsides and turns to sorrow. Sorrow at what this discussion has forced him to now do.

Kotoru's eyes grow wide as Thane unsheathes Halcyondis. For a long moment, a freezing chill runs down Kotoru's spine. Has he made an error and gravely misjudged his nephew's sense of duty and honor? Is he about to initiate the ancient Indali challenge known as the Death Challenge of the Deadly Blade, Death Blade Challenge for short. The challenge to the death is the only way for a sitting chieftain to ever be challenged for leadership of the clan and can only be done by blood kin of the chieftain. If so, it could very well be the last error he ever makes. He is not arrogant enough to think he can best Thane in any sort of physical combat.

A world of relief washes over him as Thane extends and turns the sword sideways for Kotoru to take.

He's surrendering Halcyondis. Thane's giving up his position as War Chief. He was right about the boy, after all. Kotoru would have preferred a far less threatening way of learning that, but so be it. At least he now knows precisely where the line has been drawn and can freely exploit it.

Kotoru may not be the most supremely skilled fighter in the art of combat, but he has won his share of battles and many times did it using what he believes is his greatest weapon... the art of deception. In that arena, Kotoru's skills have no equal. He exhales deeply and begins the performance of a lifetime.

"That will not be necessary."

Thane's stance does not change in the slightest.

Kotoru continues. "You're right. We have denied your sister her birthright."

This does cause a change in Thanes' stance. Once again' his uncle catches him completely off guard.

"But it isn't me who has denied it. It is our people who have denied it. That is why I need you. That is why I chose you."

Thane listens intently to his uncle.

"I can decree her name be spoken. That she be accepted everywhere. But it would be an empty gesture."

Thane's brow furrows in confusion. He lowers Halcyondis. How can the decree of your clan's chieftain be an empty gesture, Thane wonders. Kotoru takes Thanes' more relaxed stance as just the sign he was looking for to continue.

"How would you have me enforce such a decree? Would you have me post the N'Dal around the city to listen for her name to be spoken? Would you also have me order our proud Indali people to act kindly toward her? Would you order our archers to fire on anyone who didn't? Would you have our warriors detain anyone who didn't agree with you? Our city, our people, our way of life would die the same as if they were bitten by a Nisha."

Thane's mind searches for solutions to his uncle's questions? He would never take part in any attempt to subjugate his people. To do so would violate everything he believes in. The Indali people are good people. They just need to be shown the way. But how? The answer unexpectedly came from the very source that posed the original question.

"What you and I must do is change their hearts and minds,

and that takes time. Me, gradually as Chieftain. You, gradually as War Chief. Together we can bring the Indali people into the modern world. Into a world where not only can your sister proudly claim her birthright, but also be celebrated for it. Will you help me? Will you help me achieve this?"

Thane contemplates his uncle's words. He recalls the words of another former master. Steedar Master Oshi was a trainer of steedar mounted combat. She taught riding, fighting and care of steedars. She also taught her students their most valuable lesson... the Order of Choice.

Before the young ones could complete their steedar training, they were required to engage in steedar mounted combat. Knowing he was highly resistant to injury and his steedar wasn't was of great concern to young Thane. He came to care for the steedar and rationed that since his steedar stood a greater chance of injury than he did, he would engage in the combat without his steedar to keep it safe. Upon learning of this, Steedar Master Oshi took young Thane aside and told him, "When the choice is between what is best for you, what is best for those you love, and what is best for your clan... there is no choice." Young Thane understood and rode his steedar into combat that day. Thane knows what he must do and knows his decision was made the moment he earned the right to be called an Indali Warrior.


The setting sun makes for a beautiful sky across the southern region of Polemis.

Thane makes his way through Indali city on his way to the steedar stables. Along the way, thankful residents grateful for his defense of their city stop him several times.

A shopkeeper offers him an assortment of sweetened sticky treats, which Thane respectfully declines.

An armourer promises to construct a custom set of armor for him.

"I picked this basket of wild fruit just for you." a smiling elderly woman offers.

Their gestures of appreciation unfortunately do little to lift Thanes' mood. He reaches the stables and takes a deep breath before entering to share with Syn his conversation with their uncle.

Thane explains to his sister. "While I don't agree with everything uncle said, he made some arguments I had no answers for but couldn't ignore."

Syn listens but doesn't bother to look up from her work, brushing a steedar as he talks.

"There is much work that needs to be done to move our people forward. I know I can lead that change, but I will need to work with him to achieve it."

Syn stops brushing and closes her eyes. "As his War Chief."

"I know this isn't what you wanted to hear. It's not the news I hoped to be telling you and I am truly sorry for that, but I have no choice."

Thane follows Syn as she puts away her brush and walks outside. She sniffs the air.

"Think you better head back. Smells like dinner's just about ready." deadpans Syn. "The roasted boar smells especially worthy of chieftain blood. Wouldn't want you to miss out."

Syn's words make the cut that no blade could. Thane can only nod solemnly before walking away. He stops after a few steps.

"Give me time. I swear on the graves of our ancestors it will not always be like this."

Thane turns back to Syn, but she's already gone.

"I promise."

Thane turns and heads back towards the Indali castle where food and celebration are already in full swing. He would give almost anything to be fighting the Nisha again right about now.

Syn is almost a blur as she exits the city and runs through the sun setting evening. Full of anger. Full of rage. Full of sadness. Full of hurt. She needs to be somewhere, anywhere, from where she just was. Thane. Her brother. Her twin. The one person on all of Polemis she knew would never betray her. The one person who understood her. The one person who she could count on. The one person who would always have her back... no matter what. She would never make that mistake again.

Syn runs through the mountain region at top speed. She narrowly misses tripping on random rocks and other debris as she runs. She makes it all the way to a familiar cliff.

She looks across the sixty-foot lengths to the other side, then down the eight-hundred-foot lengths to the rocky bottom. Syn determinedly walks back to the spot she and Thane did earlier that morning. The same spot she began her previously almost fatal leap from.

She takes a deep breath, then sprints forward.

Twelve-foot lengths to go.

Ten-foot lengths.

Five.

Two.

Syn goes to leap and... dives out of her attempt a foot length from the edge. Syn hits the ground and safely rolls on to a stop. She rolls onto her back and lays there staring up into the sky at the three moons. Syn closes her eyes and wonders why life has failed her so.

After laying there feeling sorry for herself for a time, Syn hears the faint buzzing sound of something approaching through the air. Rohini transport ships. They're moving faster this time. She thinks they must have gotten a late start back and are trying to make up time.

Syn looks up and sees that her usual viewing spot won't work since the ships will reach it before she will. This time she will need to try a different location. She thinks if she leaves right now, she can make it to the top of one of the other ridges before the ships do. This time Syn follows the earlier example of Perangun and takes the long way around.

Syn locates several passageways that will allow her to get to her destination. As she runs through, up, and over the mountains, she realizes she's never been this far from home alone before. The reality of that makes her both anxious and excited.

Syn eventually comes across another cliff with another deep valley. This time the distance is only twenty or so foot lengths. Syn easily leaps across to the other ledge and continues on up. The mountain Syn's on seems to go on for an eternity, but she continues on until finally reaching the top ledge. She immediately feels the higher elevations, more powerful wind and cold and considers crawling back down. Syn just as quickly changes her mind upon hearing the familiar sounds of the Rohini transports approaching. Something sounds slightly different this time. Instead of coming from below her as it always has before, this one comes from above. The hum of the engines seems to have more of a growl to them. They also sound far more powerful as well.

An unfamiliar ship comes into Syn's view. It's definitely not the familiar transport ship Syn's used to seeing. This ship is something far deadlier. A Rohini Assault Ship. One of four put into service recently and so far, the only one currently on Polemis.

Twice as large and significantly more maneuverable than the standard transport ships. Its more powerful liquid spark crystal fuel engines allow it to fly higher and faster. Its twin projectile launchers protrude from the ship's starboard and port sides and can launch spark crystal clusters called Blast Crystals that explode with an impact similar to that of an Earth missile. It is a machine designed for advanced warfare... and it's heading straight for Syn.

Syn knows that if they haven't already spotted her, the rapidly approaching ship will surely spot her in moments. She panics. It's too late for her to climb back down and there's nowhere to hide on the top. She's totally exposed. Syn reaches down and grasps the underside of the rocky ledge. She moves under it, holding on for dear life.

Aboard the Rohini ship sit a pair of Rohini warriors dressed in black battle armor similar to those worn by Samurai on Earth. They are the ship's pilot and co-pilot.

Syn's movements catch the attention of the pilot. "Did you see that?"

The co-pilot looks up from his instrument panel and looks outside. "See what?"

"I thought I saw someone on the ledge down there."

"Not possible. We're over a thousand-foot lengths from ground level. No one could survive up here."

"I tell you I saw something moving around down there."

"A saberwolf maybe?" his co-pilot says after a long moment. "I've heard stories about those things."

The pilot taps his fingers on his console. "Not taking any chances."

The pilot presses a button on his console and speaks.

"Stand by for weapons test."

"Prepare to deploy projectiles." the pilot says to his co-pilot.

The copilot flips a lever on his console. A hatch opens inside each of the projectile launchers. A blast crystal drops from the hatch into each launcher.

Underneath the ledge, Syn digs her hands deeper into the mountain rock. She ignores the pain and blood dripping from the many cuts on her fingers. She wishes she could have been born with the tough skin and raw strength of her twin brother. Life strikes again, she thought.

Back onboard the ship the pilots continue preparing to fire at Syn.

"Projectiles loaded." says the co-pilot.

"Fill compressed air chambers to point two five."

The co-pilot reaches up and flips a switch on an overhead

console.

Tanks sitting behind the blast crystals fill with compressed air.

"Both chambers at point two five."

"Open compressed air valves."

The co-pilot presses a pair of buttons on the same overhead console.

Small tubes open and extend to the backs of the blast crystals.

"Valves opened."

"Target the ledge." the pilot says.

The co-pilot pushes a button on his console and starts tuning a dial.

A pair of cross-hairs appear on a screen in front of him, narrowing as he turns the dial until the ledge Syn's on is perfectly lined up in them.

"Target locked. Ready to fire." says the co-pilot.

"Almost in range. Prepare to fire on my mark."

The copilot reaches his hand over a red button ready to fire.

Inside a small room behind the pilots sits a woman who appears to be in her mid-forties and dressed in an elaborate black formal robe. Underlord Daimos stares at the long shard of glowing yellowish-orange crystal she's holding like a newly discovered long-lost treasure.

Underlord Daimos places the glowing crystal into a clear cylindrical tube and attaches the crystal to two metal leads, one at each end. The glowing yellowish-orange crystal changes color to an intense glowing red. A look of immense awe forms on the face of Underlord Daimos. She is so distracted by the glowing crystal she only partially hears the pilot announce *Stand by for weapons test*. Satisfied with her examination and test of the glowing crystal, Underlord Daimos stands and walks out of the room and through the short hallway into the pilot area.

"Hold position here." Underlord Daimos orders the pilot just as he's about to give the order to fire.

The pilot immediately throttles the ship down. The assault ship slows to a hover, stopping almost directly over Syn's position.

The concentrated vibrations of the ship's hover mode rain down on the ledge, causing micro fractures in the rocks. They cause Syn to lose her grip momentarily. She drops a couple foot lengths before grabbing hold again. The reality of the danger she's in echoes through her mind.

Syn hates her life among the Indali, hates living in the stables, hates being looked down on. She hates being hated.

A dark thought crosses her mind. I could just... let go. The thought gives her a sense of peace. A sense of calmness, in a way. A sense of control. It is a thought that has crossed her mind more times than she would like to admit. Less frequently now than it once did. Thanks, in part, to getting to take care of Perangun and a few of the other steedars. It gave her that first sense of purpose. Allowed her to feel needed on some level.

Syn wonders who would take care of them, if she let go.

Who would feed Perangun his morning wild fruits if she let go?

Who would give the temperamental Tangeama her afternoon ear rubs without getting gored by her head spikes for touching that tiny tender spot that's so sensitive, if she let go?

Her thoughts drift to her brother. Who would teach him to make his eyes change color and how to see better? Who would make fun of him about the time he broke the storehouse door looking for snacks when they were young, if she let go?

Syn decides she would miss the wonderful smells coming from the talented Indali cooks while eagerly waiting for her brother to bring her a plate. She decides she would miss her room above the stables tucked snuggly into her surprisingly rather comfortable bed. She decides she misses the safety of Indali City. Syn realizes she would give anything to be there right now. It's far from perfect, but it is home.

Maybe, she decides, she shouldn't let go.

Underlord Daimos takes out a small communication crystal. She closes her eyes and squeezes the communication crystal tightly. The communication crystal connects to its other crystal half. Though separated, the two halves link by a shared resonating frequency that can transmit a two-way visual image of the person holding one half of the crystal to the other half in a crystalized format. Concentrating on the owner of the other half of the crystal further strengthens the connection.

Underlord Daimos opens her eyes and hands to see a crystalized form of a man whose chiseled face appears to be in his late forties but is in reality many thousands of years old.

"Lord Kazini, I have news of great importance." Underlord Daimos displays the glowing red crystal shard to Lord Kazini. His crystal shaped eyes grow wide.

"Bring it to me at once." he says.

The crystalized display of Lord Kazini disappears back into the crystal.

"How far are we from Atea?" Underlord Daimos asks. "Approximately forty-five tics." answers the pilot.

"Increase speed. I wish to arrive as soon as possible so that we may depart on the next platform immediately for Volana."

The Rohini pilot nods and increases speed.

The roar of the engines shakes the mountain ledge Syn is holding on to. It begins to break apart. The sudden increase in the loudness of the engines has another unintended, but no less unfortunate, effect. The highly sensitive ears of Syn are blasted with this newly enhanced sound. She becomes disoriented and loses her grip on the mountain ledge and falls.

The scream Syn lets out as she drops is deafening. Silence replaces the sound of her scream as it tails off until being interrupted by the echoing boom of her body hitting solid rock.


Meanwhile, the Indali great hall bristles with activity. Soft colorful tunics take the place of armor, as this is a time of both rejoice and remembrance. Ayanti dances alongside the ritual dancers as they perform the traditional rhythmic bodily movements of celebration. Leto is out front, leading the drummers using goblet-shaped drums topped with animal skin to imbue the room with glorious sounds.

Succulent scents of food and drink fill the air. Roasted meats, baked breads, stewed garden vegetables, boiled wild fruits, smoked fish and a dozen fruit wines were in hearty abundance. Most Indali rarely ate food in this quantity, but tonight was a special occasion.

Thane sits by himself in a far-off corner, nursing a cup of sweet fruit wine and pushing pieces of boar and bread around his plate. His mind is elsewhere, as Kotoru stands silencing the celebration.

"Commander Thane, come before me."

All eyes turn to Thane as he stands and walks to his uncle's throne and kneels, his conflicted emotions oblivious to all but the closest of his friends.

Rumors of Kotoru's decision to appoint his nephew, War Chief, had already reached the ears of the other commanders. The very few that had any less than supportive remarks quickly silenced themselves after a stern look from Leto.

Kotoru looks down at his nephew. "Never before in the history of the Indali has one so young been appointed so high a position. But never before has one so young been as revered by his fellow warriors as you."

A brief chorus of clangs ring out from the gathered warriors banging their cups on their tables signaling their overwhelming agreement with their Chieftain.

"Commander Thane. You have shown mastery of oneself both on and off the battlefield. It is my honor and privilege to bestow upon you the title of War Chief of the Indali and the rank of General." Kotoru takes his scepter, Kotoru's chosen symbol of Indali leadership, and touches each of Thanes' shoulders. Another chorus of clangs from the warriors quickly follows.

At the moment of his greatest achievement, Thane forces his sadness, mixed feelings and split loyalties to the back of his mind so that he may perform in the way he has trained his entire life to perform... to do what is best for his clan.

"I pledge my loyalty, my honor, and my sword to defend my clan and my chieftain." The warriors clang their cups and cheer loudly.

Kotoru flashes a smug smile and bends down to whisper to his nephew.

"I intend to hold you to those words... General Thane."

Thane believes he finally understands why he never heard General Taan utter a single kind word about his uncle. He knows if change is ever going to come for his sister, for his people, or for Polemis, it starts now.

"To the last. The words General Taan would yell as he led us into battle. To the last. We shall fight until the last warrior falls. To the last. We shall fight until the last enemy falls. To the last. I am not General Taan. I do not stand before you as his replacement. To do so would be impossible. No. I stand before you as the son of a chieftain. I stand before you as the son of a War Chief. I stand before you as their hope, their dream, for a better world, a better life, for that is the birthright of all Indali people. And for that, I shall fight... to the last!!!"

Cheers abound at Thane's rousing speech.

"To the last!!!", yells Thane as he draws Halcyondis and thrusts it in the air and continues chanting.

"To the last!!!"

As the room erupts into thunderous prolonged chants of "To the last!!!", Thane turns from his right to his left and continues until he locks eyes with his uncle.

Kotoru and Thane glare at each other while the chants continue.

After the celebration ends, Thane gathers large leftover piles of boar, bread, and vegetables into a large satchel and makes his way back to the stables. He hopes this small peace offering will help make the difficult situation with his twin sister at least a little better. Thane's sense of smell tells him before he even enters that she isn't there. Where could she be, he worriedly wonders?

At the rocky base of the mountain, over one-thousand-foot lengths below the mountain ledge, lays Syn's broken dead body. Syn's dead body would appear to be completely lifeless to anyone who found her. Even Thane, with all of his heightened senses, would regard his twin sister as nothing more than a lifeless corpse right now and would be mourning heavily as he performs the Indali burial ceremony.

Inside Syn's dead body, all of her internal organs ceased functioning at the time of impact. Most have been crushed beyond recognition.

All except one.

A small gland, unique only to Syn, located at the base of her formerly intact brain, goes to work.

The gland begins secreting a thick shiny black fluid. The black fluid flows through Syn's body, coating her damaged internal organs. Her heart, lungs, brain, spleen and liver all begin to regenerate. Over the course of the night, they slowly change from looking like gobs of crushed wild fruit to fully functioning organs. Thousands of bones from sharp fragments of her femur to the left-over dust of her pulverized rib cage all restore themselves.

This astounding transformation isn't just restricted to Syn's internal body. The black regeneration fluid seeps out the pores of her skin, repairing her wounds as it flows. As her external wounds heal, the black regeneration fluid dries and hardens into gray, hard shell scabs that cover the deepest and most severe of those wounds.

Syn's eyes flare open as she gasps and inhales deeply,

coming fully back to life.

It's one-hundred eighty tics past solar midnight on Polemis. one-hundred eighty tics away from dawn. A time when most of Indali city is sound asleep. But not all. A normally empty steedar stall in back of the steeder filled stable is wide awake with activity.

"How much do you remember?" Thane asks.

In between gulps of baked bread and roasted wild boar, Syn replies "There are parts I remember clearly. Like falling. I remember the patterns in the rocks as I fell past them. The scent of my own fear as I realized I was going to die. How it felt when I hit the rocks below. The bones in my back shattering into so many pieces. I remember the exact moment my brain exploded... it was just before I took my last breath. Things after that are fuzzy. Like being everywhere and nowhere at the same time. I remember floating. I have flashes of being pulled back together. Then suddenly waking up."

The entire time Syn was recalling her experience, Thane sat wide-eyed, watching and listening like a young child being regaled with the fantastic tale of a legend, a tale told between two of the few people who would believe it.

"After a battle, I'm able to remember the exact ways everyone on the battlefield fought, smelled and sounded with complete detail, but I've experienced nothing close to what you have. It's... incredible. How do you feel?" Thane asks.

Syn looks down in thought. She smiles and looks back up at her brother. "Mostly the same, I guess. Almost like I just woke up from a long sleep. I feel stronger. More alive."

Now he understands. Thane finally understands why his uncle fears Syn so much. His twin sister has just become one of the most powerful people on the planet.

Thane laughs. "Aren't we a pair? I can't get hurt and you don't stay dead."

Thane recalls the memory of their previous conversation. "About earlier--"

Syn cuts him off before he can continue. "We're good."

"Still, I meant what I said earlier about making the changes here that need to be made. We can't truly become the people father traded his life for until we do."

Despite Syn's newfound ability, she knows nothing has really changed. Her uncle is still Chieftain. To him, and everyone else in Indali city, she's still the same undesired, unloved person she was when the day began.

"What about uncle?" she asks.

Thane contemplates Syn's question. While killing him and seizing power is the easiest way, it would also be the most foolish way. Even doing so through Death Blade Challenge would not change the hearts and minds of the people, and attempting to rule them through violence and fear is as impractical as it is personally distasteful. No, this will need to happen another way.

"Leave uncle to me." Thane says.

Syn smiles and shakes her head. "Still looking out for me, dear brother?"

"Always, last born." says Thane, as he playfully jabs Syn with his elbow.

"Only by one tic." replies Syn as she playfully jabs Thane back. "Thanks."

Thane does the Indali fist to heart salute but adds another part to it. Instead of tapping his heart once, he taps twice and points a finger at Syn. She smiles and returns the gesture.

Thane walks away, then stops and turns back to Syn.

"Hey... try to stay out of trouble."

Syn flashes a sly smile. "I always try."

The twins have experienced things no one else on Polemis could ever hope to truly understand. The two are identical in almost every way. Yet the few ways they differ will either halt Armageddon or unleash it.

High in orbit above Polemis, on its largest moon Volana, stands the towering presence of the menacing Rohini Imperial Palace.

Sitting in front of it on a partially constructed landing port, sits a trio of Rohini assault ships. Among them sits the recently landed ship of Underlord Daimos.

Underlord Daimos hurriedly strides through the massive courtyard that leads to the front of the Rohini Imperial Palace.

Training in the courtyard are one-thousand stealth assassin warriors called Tyr. Dressed head to toe in fitted all black uniforms with matching armor, the Tyr are being drilled by their commander, known only as First-Tyr, in the deadly art of Okan-Pa, an aggressive martial arts style involving bladed weapons and empty-hand combat.

The Tyr separate into two facing groups as Underlord Daimos walks the long path between them up to the Imperial Palace.

Standing on the steps of the Rohini Imperial Palace viewing the training is the imposing figure Lord Kazini, dressed in red Rohini armor.

Standing on Lord Kazini's right dressed in long black robes is a tall, haughty young man with chiseled features named Vek, Lord Kazini's son. Vek is the newly appointed Governor of Volana and heir to the Rohini throne.

On the opposite side is a younger woman with piercing eyes and an icy, severe expression named Reyhanni, Lord Kazini's daughter. Today, the ambitious Reyhanni will join the Tyr where she will undergo training to one day lead them.

Underlord Daimos walks up and hands Lord Kazini the glowing shard of crystal she had earlier. Lord Kazini takes it and holds it up.

"Behold and bear witness, my children, a shard from the Heart of Polemis."

Lord Kazini gazes into the shard. "Unlimited power."

Back on Polemis, far from Indali City, the flock of skyfish continue their long journey towards their birth home.

The strong and swift flyers pass over the arid desert region, with its many caves that serve as home to the Nisha as well as an eccentric blind old woman.

They soar to the west over the city of Avin, a place known as the "wild west" of Polemis. A place where one can enlist members of the ancient Avinashi clan known for their superior tracking skills as bounty hunters for hire.

The skyfish elevate high to pass over the dense forest region known as the Dark Woods where the small village of the fearsome hunter-gatherer clan known as the Da'ku attempt to etch out an existence guided by their revered warrior High Priestess. Unfortunately for the Da'ku, the Dark Woods are also home to the cannibalistic Ekani clan and roaming packs of the apex predator Saberwolves.

The skyfish dive to avoid the northern artic air of Naija, the uninhabited ice-covered northern pole of Polemis.

They gain speed and continue south, past the scarred city of Kenetica, where the last remnant of the once mighty Blood Noble Monarchy now calls their home.

The long journey of the flock finally comes to an end as they reach their destination, Antak, the equatorial center of the planet and the birthplace of life on Polemis, to lay their eggs and continue their line.

The dawn of a new day is almost upon the inhabitants of the southern region of Polemis. It will be the first day in a while that won't involve the bandaging of battle wounds, the burning of dead and withering bodies, and the mourning of their kin. Before the sun rises over the horizon, early risers, non-sleepers and the newly awakened stir about the city.

Kotoru stands on the battlement, staring up at the three moons. He smiles, determined to achieve the power and influence he's long sought.

Thane walks the perimeter of Indali city for the first of what will be many times. On his hip is Halcyondis emblazoned for the first time with the name Thane. He is now known to all as General Thane, War Chief of the Indali. The next chapter of his book has been written. It will be far from the last.

Syn lays sleeping in her room at the stables when she hears a faint dreamy voice in her mind say "Dey-ko-ma-syn". Syn awakens quickly from her dream. She's drenched in sweat and her heart feels like it's beating through her chest.

The language Syn hears in her dream is a language she has not heard since speaking it with Thane when they were children. The twins believe it to be a language they made up, never knowing they were speaking the ancient Kalayman language. Her innate understanding of the language allows Syn to translate "Dey-ko-ma-syn" to mean "and her name was Death."

On Earth, this would be but a mere dream. A nightmare one would soon forget as you go about your day. On Earth, a dream is simply a dream. But this is not Earth... this is Polemis, and on Polemis, dreams often become nightmares for the living.

# GLOSSARY

**Antak** (AN-tac): The equatorial center of the planet and the birthplace of life on Polemis.

**Atea City** (AT-e-uh): A technologically advanced city founded by the Blood Noble Monarchy that is now controlled by the Rohini. The city itself sits inside of a gigantic mountain that cannot be seen from the ground below.

**Avin** (AVIN): A city in the western region of Polemis created by the Avinashi clan. A place where one can enlist members' bounty hunters for hire. Known as the "wild west" of Polemis for its penchant for violence and lawlessness.

**Avinashi Clan** (AH-vin-osh-ee): An ancient and formerly highly respected clan, now known only for their superior tracking skills as bounty hunters for hire.

**Ayanti** (ā-yan-tee): Indali warrior commander. The fearless and loyal friend of Thane and Ayanti. Known for being merciless during sparring sessions. Enjoys dancing with the ritual dancers.

**Banhi Clan** (BON-he): A clan of fire worshippers living in the western region of Polemis.

**Blast Crystal**: Spark crystals clustered together to form a launchable projectile with the explosive characteristics of a guided missile.

**Blood Nobles**: The Blood Noble Monarchy were once the ruling power of Polemis. Comprised of nine cities each ruled by a King with one serving as High King for a century then rotating in cyclic order.

**Blood War**: The yearlong war between a coalition of nomadic clans and the Blood Noble Monarchy.

**Bor** (BOAR): A former Indali crystal farmer who fought alongside Revanche and later became a warrior and adviser with the Indali

during the Blood War. Died during the
Battle of Sangmoria.

**Chieftain**: The title of the leader of a clan on Polemis. Line of succession is usually the oldest sibling or adult child of the previous chieftain. Must be a blood kin descendant of a previous chieftain to rule as leader.

**Communication Crystal**: A crystal-based form of communication where separated halves of the same crystal can be used for communication via a shared resonating frequency that can transmit a two-way visual image of the person holding one half of the crystal to the other half in a crystalized format. Concentrating on the receiver by sender further strengthens the connection.

**Da'ku Clan** (DA-ku): A clan of hunter-gatherers led by their High Priest and Priestess. Were slaughtered by the Blood Nobles during an attempted seizure of their lands in an action that contributed to the start of the Blood War. Also, a small clan of fierce hunter-gatherers living in the Dark Woods are also known as the Da'ku. They are led by their revered warrior High Priestess and may be an offshoot of the original Da'ku.

**Death Blade Challenge**: An ancient Indali challenge also known as the Death Challenge of the Deadly Blade. The challenge to the death is the only way for a sitting chieftain to ever be challenged for leadership of the clan and can only be done by blood kin of the chieftain.

**Ekani Clan** (E-con-e): A clan of cannibals that inhabit the Dark Woods region of Polemis.

**Foot-Length**: A unit of measurement equivalent to one foot on Earth.

**Halcyondis** (HAL-see-ahn-diss): The ancient golden sword wielded by all past and present Indali War Chiefs.

**Heart of Polemis**: A glowing yellowish-orange crystal that, when connected with certain metals, changes color to an intense glowing red that is rumored to emit unlimited power.

**Indali Castle**: The fortified home of Indali Chieftain Kotoru.

Formerly called Sangmoria Palace.

**Indali City**: The fortified city of the Indali Clan. Formerly called Sangmoria City.

**Indali Clan** (IN-doll-e): A powerful warrior clan based in the southern region of Polemis. Fought alongside the other coalition clans against the Blood Noble Monarchy in the Blood War. Launched a clan wide assault on the weakened Blood Nobles weeks after their chieftain Revanche was executed, resulting in victory in the Battle of Sangmoria, the ending battle of the Blood War.

**Kalayman** (KUH-lay-men): The ancient language of the nomadic people of Polemis. Other than its appearance on some ancient cave walls and artifacts, and can somehow by spoken and translated by Syn and Thane, it is a dead language on Polemis.

**Kazini** (KA-ze-ne): Also known as Kazini the Usurper. Warlord of the Rohini Clan and creator of The Three Moons triumvirate. Rose to clan lord by executing the entire family of the previous Rohini chieftain. A fanatical worshipper and scholar of the ancient Polemini moon spirits.

**Kenetica** (KEN-e-she-uh): The last surviving city of the Blood Noble Monarchy.

**Kor'vai** (CORE-vay): The gray skinned, ancient and diminutive Nisha brood Queen. A veteran battlefield tactician.

**Kotoru** (KO-tor-ru): Chieftain of the Indali. Uncle of Thane and Syn. Younger brother of Revanche. The stout, brutish and grizzled older man with calculating eyes is determined to achieve the power and influence he's long sought by any means necessary.

**Kytara** (KY-tar-uh): Former War Chief of the Indali. Mate of Revanche. Mother of Thyrox, Thane and Syn. An amazing warrior, renowned sword master and strategist. Plotted many of the coalition of nomadic clans most daring campaigns during the Blood War. Killed during the Blood War, presumably at the hands of the Blood Nobles in Sangmoria City

**Leto** (LEE-toe): Indali warrior commander. The gregarious and deep baritone friend of Thane and Ayanti. An accomplished drummer.

**Lokeer** (LOW-k-ear): A member of the Indali war council and friend of Revanche who fought alongside him in the Blood War. Died during the war.

**Marana** (MAR-ah-nuh): The smallest of the three moons of Polemis. Home of the Satvari Clan.

**Master Oshi** (O-she): Master trainer of steedar mounted combat.

**Me'nar** (ME-nar): A member of the Indali war council and friend of Revanche who fought alongside him in the Blood War. Died during the war.

**Micro-Tics**: A unit of time equivalent to one second on Earth.

**N'Dal** (NUH-doll): The personal guards of Chieftain Kotoru. They are separate and independent of the warrior class of the Indali.

**Naija** (NAY-juh): The uninhabited ice-covered northern pole of Polemis.

**Nisha Clan** (NISH-uh): A clan of humanoid night worshippers that inhabit the southern region of Polemis but have hunting grounds all over the planet. Riding on giant nocturnal mammals called Petaurus, the sinewy gray hued beings hunt at night, avoid sunlight and wear mouth harnesses with metal fangs dipped in a parasitic poison. Their diet comprises fresh fish, wild boar and blood.

**Niyati Clan** (NEE-yat-e): Led by Lady Niyati VII. Inhabitants of Osupa, a moon of Polemis. A founding member of The Three Moons triumvirate. Responsible for the crystal weapon program.

**Okan-Pa** (OKAN-pa): An aggressive style of martial arts used by the Tyr involving bladed weapons and empty-hand combat.

**Osupa** (O-supe-uh): The second largest of the three moons of Polemis. Home of the Niyati Clan.

**Perangun** (PER-ang-un): Thane's trusty red steedar who love to run and snack on wild fruit.

**Petaurus** (PET-ar-us): Nocturnal mammals with enormous eyes, prehensile tails and gliding membranes. Used by the Nisha to travel to and from their hunting grounds.

**Polemini Moon Spirits**: Lunar deities representing the three moons of Polemis that were once worshipped by ancient nomadic clerics. Although not widely accepted, a small group of true-believers came to power among the Rohini led by the ancestors of Lord Kazini who prophesied the Rohini would live on Volana and conquer Polemis.

**Polemis** (PO-lem-iss): A large planet with three moons that is home to an array of humans, humanoids and animals.

**Rattan** (RA-Tan): The long-time aide and advisor to Kotoru.

**Revanche** (RAY-von-shh): Former Indali Chieftain. Mate of Kytara. Father of Thyrox, Thane and Syn. Organized and led the coalition of nomadic clans in the yearlong Blood War against the Blood Noble Monarchy after the death of his son Thyrox and the slaughter of the Da'ku clan. Surrendered to the Blood Nobles after the death of Kytara in an effort to end the war and spare his people. He was executed soon after.

**Reyhanni** (RAY-haun-e): Lord Kazini's young daughter and the younger sister of Vek.

**Rohini Clan** (ROW-e-knee): A ruthless, technologically advanced and powerful clan led by Lord Kazini. Inhabitants of Volana, a moon of Polemis and controllers of Atea City on Polemis. A founding member of The Three Moons triumvirate.

**Rukai** (RUE-kai): A former Indali bladesmith and friend of Kytara who fought alongside her in the Blood War.

**Saberwolves** (SAY-bur-wolves): Large predatory lupine carnivores with amber-colored eyes and two sets of long, thick razor-sharp canine teeth. They roam the Dark Woods region in packs of six and are led by an even larger Alpha and it's usually more aggressive mate.

**Sangmoria** (SANG-more-ee-uh): The former capital city of the Blood Noble Monarchy. Invaded by the coalition of nomadic clans during the Blood War where they made it all the way to

Sangmoria Palace. Sangmoria Palace remained under siege for three months before the invading leader, Revanche, surrendered to the Blood Noble High King Soranus. The city and palace later fell to the Indali led by General Taan during the Battle of Sangmoria. It is now known as Indali City.

**Sanguinos** (SANG-win-us): The territorial lands of the Indali where Indali City is located. Formerly called Sangmoria.

**Sateea** (SA-tee-uh): A former Da'ku hunter and older cousin of Vorii. Fought alongside Revanche during the Blood War after Blood Nobles slaughtered her clan. Died during the war.

**Satvari Clan** (SAT-var-e): Led by Lord Dekeda. Inhabitants of Marama, a moon of Polemis. A founding member of The Three Moons triumvirate. Renowned for their shipbuilding skills.

**Skyfish** (SKY-fish): Tiny white-winged creatures that can exist either in the air or in the water. Every five years, they fly across Polemis to their spawning grounds in Antak.

**Spark Crystal**: Red crystals that, when struck together, create an intense and highly combustible spark capable of incinerating flesh.

**Steedars** (STEE-ders): Tail-less four-legged riding animals with a row of sharp bones protruding from their head and body used by the Indali.

**Syn** (SIN): Indali stable girl. Niece of Kotoru. Twin sister of Thane. The son of former Indali Chieftain Revanche and War Chief Kytara. The reviled and scorned stable girl born with superhuman speed and senses has only scratched the surface of her amazing abilities.

**Taan** (TAN): General and War Chief of the Indali Warriors. Mentor and surrogate father figure of Thane. A veteran of many wars and conflicts, including the Blood War and Nisha raids. Led the Indali clan to victory in the Battle of Sangmoria, the ending battle of the Blood War.

**Thane** (Thān): Indali warrior commander. Twin brother of Syn. Nephew of Kotoru. The son of former Indali Chieftain Revanche and War Chief Kytara. Born with superhuman strength, speed, reflexes, agility, eyesight, hearing and smell. Nigh-invulnerable. The fearless and highly intelligent Thane is beloved by the Indali people and fated to one day unite the clans and lead them to victory over their greatest enemy, as decreed by his father.

**The Three Moons**: The triumvirate comprising the Rohini, Niyati and Satvari clans that have combined their knowledge and resources to one day conquer and subjugate all of Polemis for their own separate reasons.

**The Tyr** (TEAR): Deadly stealth assassin warriors dressed head to toe in fitted, all black uniforms with matching armor.

**Thyrox** (THIGH-rocks): The first son of Thane and Kytara. Killed by the Blood Nobles in retaliation for starting an uprising and interfering in the forced removal of Da'ku nomads from newly seized lands. His death resulted in Revanche gathering allies and declaring war on the Blood Nobles (Blood War).

**Tics**: A unit of time equivalent to one minute on Earth.

**Underlord Daimos** (DIE-mos): One of four Underlords of Lord Kazini. Assigned to each of the four quadrants of Polemis, they serve as Lord Kazini's eyes, ears, voice and fist on the planet. Daimos is assigned to the quadrant consisting of the southern and desert regions of the planet.

**Vek** (VEK): Lord Kazini's son and older brother of Reyhanni.

**Volana** (VO-La-nuh): The largest of the three moons of Polemis. It is a moon rich in precious metals and crystals. Home to the Rohini Clan.

**Vorii** (VOR-ree): The young daughter of the deceased High Priest and Priestess of the original Da'ku who were slaughtered by the Blood Nobles along with most of the Da'ku clan. Joined and fought alongside Revanche during the Blood War, where she developed a reputation for viciously slaughtering Blood Nobles. Disappeared along with dozens of others during the waning stages of the war and was presumed dead.

**War Chief**: The appointed military leader of a clan on Polemis. The adult sibling or child of the current chieftain. Usually given the title of General upon being appointed.

# ABOUT THE AUTHOR

Tia Cherie Polite, a native of Washington, DC, is an author, filmmaker/director, screenwriter and VFX artist. Tia has been involved in some form of creative arts for many years. Her deep love of sci-fi, fantasy, and action are always at the forefront of her work. Tia's stories are told in the spirit of wars fought in the stars and of great houses fighting on desert dunes. In her free time, Tia enjoys cooking, watching football, and watching TV and movies with her husband.

BLOOD/CLAN: Harbinger of Death is Tia's first novel and is a part of the BLOOD/CLAN universe created by her. She plans to continue making stories from yesterday told for today by creating and expanding the BLOOD/CLAN saga.
Visit her website at www.tiacheriepolite.com.